Father Roberto and the Runaway Ring

Two heartwarming cosy mysteries

Stefania Hartley

THE*SICILIAN*MAMA

ALSO AVAILABLE AS
EBOOK AND LARGE PRINT

ISBN: 978-1-914606-59-5

Edited by Sandy Salisbury

Cover illustration and design by
Joseph Witchall
https://josephwitchall.com/

To my parish priest.

CONTENTS

1. THE RUNAWAY RING

When Father Roberto thought of the kingdom of God, he usually imagined one of those Sicilian summer's days when the sky was cobalt blue and the sun filled the church with light.

Today was a day just like that, Roberto thought as he stood at the top of the church's steps. He had just finished celebrating the early morning Mass with those parishioners who liked to be back home before the day got too hot.

The gospel reading had been about a vineyard owner who went to the town's square to hire workers for his vineyard. Despite hiring people at different times of the day, he had then paid everyone a full day's wages. Roberto always struggled to comment on that story. He found it hard to concentrate on the generosity of the vineyard owner rather than on the unfairness of the deal. Maybe he needed to learn to be more generous himself, he thought.

Roberto looked out on the square in front of the church. There was the usual little crowd of teenagers loitering on their bicycles and scooters—chatting, doing wheelies, kicking a football about.

One of them was Tano. A self-professed black sheep of his family, the nineteen-year-old was older than the other kids on the square, who were on school holiday. As far as Roberto knew, Tano had left school a while ago. Surely he should be working or looking for work, Roberto thought.

As soon as Tano saw Roberto, he revved up his scooter and zoomed to the bottom of the steps. "Hello, Father!"

"Hello, Tano."

"Have you finished saying Mass?"

"I have. Why don't you join Mass some time, as you're already here?"

Tano shook his head. "I'm too busy."

"Busy with what?" Roberto asked, hoping the question didn't sound confrontational or disapproving.

"Hanging out with the other kids…" Tano shifted uncomfortably on his saddle, "I know I'm too old to goof around with them, but I don't want to do the things that boys my age do."

"What do they do?" Roberto asked innocently.

Tano looked over his shoulders. "They work for Ciccio Titotto or Tonio Moneta." Tano lowered his voice when he said the names of the two local criminal bosses.

"Then I'm very glad that you're not doing that. But what about some honest work?"

"Where is that?" Tano opened his arms in resignation. "We haven't got any work here and I don't want to emigrate to Milan or Turin. I can't leave my nonna. She needs me." He checked his phone. "In fact, she's just texted me to go home. She needs help to open a tin of tuna. With her arthritis, she can't grip things anymore. I have to do a lot of her housework for her," Tano said.

"If you're living together, then it's not 'her' housework. It's yours too."

Tano looked a little confused. "Whatever you say, Father. I have to go. Goodbye."

"Goodbye, Tano."

Roberto watched the young man ride off and felt a pang of sympathy for him. Father Pietro had told him about Tano's story—how his parents had abandoned him and his grandma had brought him up on her own— and Roberto felt for the young man.

He wished he could give Tano a job and a

future away from the clutches of the neighbourhood's criminals, but Roberto was no vineyard owner. All he could so was pray the heavenly vineyard owner to send help.

*****

The parish included mostly poorer homes but also a handful of patrician villas. Once the summer residences of Palermo's nobility, these mansions were no longer surrounded by vineyards and olive groves but had been engulfed by the expanding city.

Signora Petronia Albi owned a beautiful villa not far from the church, and was one of Roberto's wealthiest parishioners.

"Hello, Father," she greeted him as she walked into the vestry after Mass. "Have you got a moment?"

"Sure. If you wait at the confessional, I'll be with you in a moment," Roberto replied.

"Actually, I haven't come for confession. I need your help," she said. "Do you know any honest, hardworking girl who's looking for a job? I need a new housekeeper. I had to let my previous one go because I lost trust in her— she was borrowing my clothes without permission. If you could recommend a diligent, honest girl, I would be very grateful."

"I can't think of anyone but I will ask Father Pietro," Roberto said, then suddenly had an idea. "Actually, I do! Does it have to be a girl?"

"No. Any age will do."

"I mean, how about a boy?" Roberto asked hopefully. This could be the answer to his prayers.

"A boy housekeeper?" Signora Albi repeated in disbelief.

"Yes. I have a very honest young man in mind. He lives with his grandma and does a lot of domestic chores."

"Can he clean?"

"Yes," Roberto replied confidently. Tano had told him that he did a lot of the housework.

"Is he a good cook?"

All Roberto knew about Tano's cooking abilities was that he could open tins of tuna, but he wanted Tano to get this job. "Absolutely."

Signora Albi still looked unconvinced. "I've never heard of a male housekeeper."

"But you've surely heard of male butlers. The two roles can overlap," Roberto pointed out.

Signora Albi shook her head. "Fine. If you recommend this young man, I'll give him a chance. Just because I trust you."

"Thank you!"

Roberto rushed to give Tano the good news.

***

As usual, Tano was out on the square with

his scooter. Roberto called him over and, once they were out of earshot of the other kids, gave him the good news.

Tano's eyes widened. "Tell me you're joking!"

"I'm totally serious."

"With all respect, Father, I'm not doing it!" The teen folded his arms.

"Why? It's an honest job."

"It's a job for girls."

"Who says so? Guys have arms, legs and brains just like the girls do. You can do it."

Tano hitched his scooter onto its stand, got off and paced around it. "I'm not wearing a pinafore."

"You don't have to. Does Mr Muscle wear an apron on the bottles of cleaning products?"

"No, he doesn't," Tano admitted.

Roberto thought it was encouraging that the teen was familiar with cleaning products.

"So the answer is yes?" Roberto asked hopefully.

Tano sighed. "Okay."

"Great. May I suggest that you spend the next few days learning all your nonna's best recipes?"

"What? I'm going to have to cook as well?"

Roberto nodded.

"No way!"

"Why? Don't tell me that cooking is a job for girls because there are plenty of male chefs."

"I know. I've seen them on TV."

So Tano watched cookery programmes. This was another encouraging piece of information.

"But I can't learn everything in a few days," Tano continued.

"You can learn enough to start then job, then you can continue learning. Look, Tano: this is a good job with all the paperwork in order—including insurance and pension contributions. It will look go on your CV and change your future."

"Jesus said not to worry about the future. Only worry about today," Tano retorted.

Roberto smiled. "Fair point. Then let's forget about your future and let's think about my present. I've just recommended you to Signora Albi. My reputation is at stake."

Tano's expression softened and Roberto was touched that the young man cared about him.

"Then I will have to do my best, Father," Tano replied seriously. "When do I start?"

"On Monday."

"Then I'd better go home and get Nonna to show me all her secret recipes."

Roberto patted him on the back. "Good choice, Tano."

***

The singing lessons he had had in the seminary hadn't made Roberto a good singer. They had just made his teacher more patient.

Roberto struggled with low notes as well as with high ones, found melodies a mystery, and had no idea how to keep a constant beat.

He consoled himself with the thought that it was better to have little control over one's larynx than over one's tongue, and happily left his parishioners in charge of singing the hymns.

But this evening the person who usually started the singing wasn't in church. When Roberto started walking down the aisle towards the altar, nobody started to sing. Roberto's steps echoed painfully in the silent nave. In desperation, Roberto began to sing the entrance song.

To his relief, everyone immediately joined in, but it soon appeared that he had pitched it too low for the predominantly female congregation. As one by one the congregation dropped out of the song, Roberto was left singing on his own. It was a pitiful sound and Roberto didn't attempt any other hymns for the rest of the celebration.

Afterwards, Roberto headed to one of the

meeting rooms for the marriage preparation course.

The sessions were run by Agostino and Maria—an inspiring couple from the parish—but today it was Roberto's turn to speak. Roberto had diligently prepared his notes and felt ready to deliver his speech to the engaged couples.

When he walked into the room, Agostino and Maria were already there and all the chairs were taken by the couples, except for two empty chairs.

"Giovanni and Clara are late," Maria explained.

"As usual," Agostino added. "We'd better start without them."

So Roberto greeted the other couples and began his talk about the difference between civil and religious marriage.

Half an hour later, the missing couple walked into the room and plonked themselves into the empty chairs.

"Roberto, these are Giovanni and Clara," Agostino and Maria introduced them.

"Welcome," Roberto greeted them warmly.

They replied with a mere nod and, as soon as Roberto resumed the talk, they got their phones out of their pockets.

Roberto had never seen anyone so blatantly

uninterested in what he had to say. It was a little disheartening.

Then it was time for the couples to discuss Roberto's questions between them. Giovanni and Clara continued to look at their phones.

"Don't take it personally," Maria whispered to Roberto. "Giovanni and Clara are always like that. They remind me of those kids who've been forced by their parents to attend catechism classes."

"Are you saying that Giovanni and Clara might have been pressured to have a church wedding?" Roberto asked.

"I wouldn't rule it out. Parents can put a lot of pressure on a couple at any age," Maria said sadly. "This is why we devote a whole session of the marriage preparation course to detachment from the families of origin."

If this was the case for Giovanna and Clara, a religious wedding would be meaningless, Roberto thought. He wasn't going to play along with such a sham.

At the end of the session, Roberto caught up with Giovanni and Clara as they were leaving. "May I have a word?"

"Sorry we were late, Father. We finished work late," Clara apologised.

"It's not about the lateness. I'd just like to ask you some questions."

The couple exchanged a worried look. "We've got to dash off but we promise we'll be on time for the next session."

"Then can we have a word some time this week?" Roberto pressed on.

"Sure. We'll come early before the next session."

Roberto didn't hold much hope that they would keep their word but he couldn't hold them back now. He would have to be smarter and catch them at some other time.

***

It was one of those Sicilian summer days when the wind and the sunlight make your eyes sting.

Roberto had hung the laundry out on the church's roof to dry and had returned to his room to read. Just one chapter of "Introduction to the Devout Life" later, the laundry was all dry and stiff like cardboard.

Poor Father Pietro wasn't going to be happy. He didn't like his towels to feel like cardboard. He had often suggested he should look after the laundry, but Roberto resisted giving it up.

He loved going up on the roof and bathing in the sunlight reflecting off the whitewashed walls. He always lingered to admire the view of Palermo's roofs. To the North-East was the sea, blue and glittering, with a cruise ship docked in the harbour. To the North, Monte Pellegrino looked down on Palermo benevolently, with its sanctuary of Saint Rosalia, patron saint of the city. Over there were the red domes of the Arab-Norman churches. Here the cathedral's belltower and the green and golden tiled domes reflecting the light.

This rooftop terrace was his own private space, Roberto thought, where nobody else went or would think of looking for him.

Just as he was thinking that, the door squeaked. Signora Albi stepped into the light with the darkest of scowls. She marched up to him.

"I know what you were trying to do. You thought you'd do a good deed to the boy. But you've done a bad deed to me. I shouldn't have listened to you," she said, pointing her finger at his chest.

Roberto stepped back. "What happened?"

Had Tano burned the ironing? Had he charred the dinner? Maybe he had smashed a precious vase. Poor boy, Roberto thought with a swell of sympathy and sadness.

"Your young man has stolen my grandmother's engagement ring—not only a very valuable jewel, but also a family heirloom.

One which my Filippo was planning to give to his girlfriend next Sunday, when he was going to propose. And now he can't propose until the ring is returned," Signora Albi said indignantly.

"What makes you think that Tano stole it?"

Roberto couldn't imagine Tano doing anything like that. If he wished to be a criminal, he had plenty more lucrative options with the local bosses.

"I'm absolutely certain that he did it. He was the last person in that room before the ring went missing."

"Have you talked to him?" Roberto asked, still unconvinced.

"I'm not getting into an argument with a petty thief. You recommended him to me so you must get the ring out of him. I hold you fully responsible for his crimes. I want the ring back before Sunday lunchtime or I'll go to the police. My husband is a lawyer and will make sure that both the boy and you end up in jail."

With that, she stormed back down the stairs.

Roberto decided that the laundry could sunbathe a little longer. He had to go and talk to Tano immediately.

***

Tano and his nonna lived in a rickety old flat on the second floor of an ancient three-storey building. The stone steps of the staircase were so worn and uneven that climbing them made you slightly seasick.

Roberto knocked on the door and Tano's nonna opened with a frown.

Without greeting Roberto, she shouted over her shoulder, "Gaetano! Your priest is here!"

Roberto had never heard Tano being called with his full Christian name. This didn't bode well.

"Have you any idea what happened to him? He won't come out of his room," she asked Roberto.

"I'll see what I can do," Roberto replied, avoiding answering her question.

If Tano hadn't told his nonna about Signora Albi's accusations, Roberto wouldn't either. If the ring was found quickly, his nonna would never have to know.

Roberto followed her down a narrow corridor through a small but impeccably kept flat. She opened the door of Tano's bedroom without knocking, and invited Roberto into what looked like an empty room.

"He's under the bed," she explained before closing the door behind Roberto.

"Tano, it's me, Father Roberto."

A faint sobbing came from under the low bedframe, but no instruction to go away and leave him alone. So Roberto sat on the floor and peered under the bed. Tano was lying on his front, facing the wall.

"I've lost the job you gave me," Tano sobbed.

"I didn't give it to you. Signora Albi did. Tell me what happened."

"I don't know what happened. I didn't do anything."

"Signora Albi thinks that you've stolen her nonna's ring."

"I haven't! I've never even seen that ring!"

Tano turned and inched out. Roberto could now see his face—red and wet with tears.

"I would never steal someone's nonna's ring. Everyone says I'm stupid, but I'm not that stupid. I swear it to God, Father, I'm innocent!"

"There's no need to swear. I believe you."

"But Signora Albi doesn't. She will tell the police, they'll put me in jail and my nonna is going to die of a broken heart. Why did this have to happen to me?" Tano sobbed.

"None of this will happen because you and I are going to find that ring," Roberto reassured him. "But you must get out from under your bed and help me, because we've only got until Sunday."

Tano shuffled out from under the bed and wiped his tears. "So you will help me?"

"Of course," Roberto replied.

Not least because he felt responsible for Tano's situation. If he hadn't insisted that Tano accepted the job, the young man wouldn't be facing theft charges.

"Signora Albi wants to put me in jail too," Roberto told him with a wry smile.

Tano beamed. "Then we would be there together!"

***

Once Tano had been reassured, had used a tissue and had drunk some water, Roberto asked him to recount exactly everything that had happened that morning.

"I started with the food shopping. I went to the market with the money Signora Albi had given me and I bought all I needed for lunch and dinner. I counted the change carefully, Father, and I made sure I wasn't cheated by the sellers. Then I came home and put the money on the kitchen counter, and the food in the fridge. Then I made the beds and did a bit of dusting. When I finished, I went back to the kitchen to start preparing lunch. That's when Signora came home, stormed into the kitchen with a face like thunder, and shouted that I had stolen her ring. I felt like bursting into tears, Father—I swear I did."

Roberto didn't doubt that for a moment,

and wondered if that had convinced Signora of his guilt.

Tano's eyes were filling with tears again at the thought. "I told her that I didn't know what she was talking about but she didn't believe me. She said that the ring had been in her jewellery box until that morning and it wasn't there anymore. If I didn't find it and give it back to her immediately, she would tell the police." Tano's chin quivered. "But I had nothing to give her. I emptied my pockets in front of her but she told me that I was fired and I should leave immediately. I was very angry and upset. I rode home really fast."

Roberto couldn't bear thinking about that last detail—he had seen Tano ride hair-raisingly fast even when he wasn't angry.

"Was there anyone else in Signora Albi's house that morning?" Roberto asked him.

"Apart from the family, no."

"Could anyone have come into the house without you noticing—for example, through a patio door or a ground floor window?"

"Yes. Rosalia from the dry-cleaning shop came to the house. She said she had to pick up Signora's dry cleaning but Signora was out and she hadn't given it to me. The rest of the family was out too."

"So you sent Rosalia away?"

"No. Rosalia said that she knew which dress Signora wanted dry cleaned because she had cleaned it before. She said she could find it if she looked. And she did. She found it."

Roberto's heart sank. "Do you mean that she went into Signora's room to look for the dress?"

"Yes."

"Please, tell me that you didn't leave her alone."

"Why not?" Tano replied defensively. "I've known Rosalia for ages. We were at school together. It's true that she works at the dry cleaner's."

Roberto sighed. "What you did was very unwise."

Tano looked at his feet in embarrassment. "I was busy in the kitchen. It's not easy to cook a nice meal for posh people," he said defensively.

"Well, what's done is done, now. At least now we know where to look for the ring."

"You don't mean that she stole the ring, do you?"

"Unless you stole it, I can't see any other possibility."

"What a cheating liar! Let's go and get the ring back!" Tano cried, standing up.

"Let's not judge too quickly. There could still be another explanation for the ring's disappearance. But we should certainly have a chat with Rosalia."

"Let's go now!"

Roberto checked his watch. "Sorry, I can't."

It was already time to go back and celebrate evening Mass. Tomorrow he had parish office duties and visits to homebound parishioners.

He couldn't let Tano look for the ring on his own, and yet he was fully booked up for the rest of the week. He needed to call for help.

***

Roberto hated asking favours from his brother, but at this time of year all the other priests he could call on were either taking a summer break or were already covering for someone else.

After years at the Vatican Observatory, studying stars and galaxies, Corrado probably didn't remember much about running a parish, Roberto reasoned, but at least his work at the Observatory was relatively flexible so he should be able to drop it and come down to Palermo to cover Roberto's parish duties for a few days.

"It's only until this Sunday," Roberto pleaded.

"Whether it's until Sunday or until next month, I must still check my diary. I can't tell a comet to come back next week just because my brother needs help," Corrado replied loftily.

"Then, if you can't help me, can you ask someone else there?"

Roberto pushed out of his mind the unkind thought that he would actually prefer someone else.

"Roberto, I haven't said that I can't help you. And anyway, my colleagues here are some of the brightest astronomy luminaries. They don't 'help out' in parishes. Just calm down and wait a moment."

Roberto shut up and waited.

"Uhm…I'm expecting a visit from a very important bishop…"

Roberto felt that the words "important" and "bishop" were not made to go together, as church leaders were supposed to be servants, but he wasn't going to argue with his brother when asking for help.

"…but he hasn't given me a date yet," Corrado continued, "so I suppose I could help you."

"Thank you!"

"Anyway, you still haven't told me why you need help so urgently. Have you got yourself into some kind of trouble again?"

Roberto bristled. "When have I ever got into trouble and asked for your help?"

"How about when you got stuck in the

chestnut tree in Nonna's orchard? Or when you smashed those bottles of passata Mamma had put aside for the winter? Or—"

"Okay, I got the gist," Roberto interrupted. "I just need to help a friend," he said vaguely.

He'd rather his brother didn't know the details of the situation. Corrado didn't need any more reasons to tease him.

"I see," Corrado said with a condescending sigh. "I've always told you that you're too tender-hearted."

***

From the moment Roberto had picked him up from the station, Corrado hadn't stopped complaining. The streets were dirty, the people were grumpy, the traffic was scary.

He complained about being picked up on a scooter and told Roberto that he should try harder to pass his car driving test.

Roberto tried not to take the criticism personally—even when it was personal—and to remind himself that his brother had dropped everything to come over from Rome and help him.

"We have to share a bathroom?" Corrado asked with surprise when Roberto showed him the presbytery's flat.

Roberto felt that it was already a great luxury that he and his brother didn't have to share a room. Corrado was also taken aback by the presbytery's lack of a dishwasher and air conditioning.

It was only when they sat down to a delicious supper of Father Pietro's spaghetti with aubergine pesto that Corrado was finally happy.

Father Pietro was very intrigued by Corrado's work at the Vatican Observatory, and all through the meal, the two of them discussed stars, both in the sky and in the Roman curia.

Roberto wasn't in the least interested in either, and couldn't help feeling that he must be an unsatisfactory sibling for his brother.

***

For a shop that purveyed cleanliness, the appearance of the dry-cleaning shop was disappointing.

The outside was grimy with soot, the signage was damaged, and a faded sticker with the shop's prices barely clung onto the inside of the window.

Roberto marvelled at the stinginess of wealthy people like Signora Albi, who could surely afford a better dry cleaner than that.

"I'm sorry, Rosalia isn't here today," the woman in the shop told Roberto and Tano. "She's gone on holiday."

Roberto's heart sank. If Rosalia had run off with the ring, this was very bad news.

One ring didn't seem enough to run away with, but if Rosalia had had unfettered access to Signora Albi's jewellery box—as Tano's story suggested—she might have stolen more than a ring. Signora Albi might have just not noticed yet.

"What do you want from her?" the shopkeeper asked suspiciously.

"I want to speak to her," Tano said, to Roberto's surprise.

Inexplicably, this seemed to soften the woman. "Oh, well, she won't have left yet. She must be at home, packing. Why don't you go and see her? But if I were you, I would hurry."

Roberto was in complete agreement with that.

They thanked the woman and stepped out of the shop.

"If you knew where Rosalia lives, why haven't we gone straight there?" Roberto asked Tano.

"I don't like going to her house. Her mum doesn't like me."

Roberto was curious to know why but he suspected the answer wouldn't be straightforward, and they didn't have time for digressions. If Rosalia was about to leave the country with Signora Alba's jewels, they needed to catch her before she stepped onto her plane.

Tano straddled his scooter and shuffled forward on the saddle. "Jump on, Father."

Roberto wasn't at all sure about riding pillion with Tano. Roberto had seen Tano ride. It had looked scary enough from a distance. He couldn't imagine being on the saddle with him.

"Is it too far to go on foot?" Roberto ventured.

"We'll be quicker on my scooter."

"I don't doubt that." Which was precisely the problem.

For the ring's sake he resigned himself to a hair-raising ride and climbed on.

"I'll go carefully," Tano reassured him.

As the cobblestones whizzed under his feet, Roberto wondered what not-careful riding would be like, and felt acutely aware of his mortality.

If he and Tano died now, while they were under suspicion of theft, they would be unlikely to be remembered in a good light.

Tano skidded to a halt in front of a two-storey building. As Roberto climbed off the scooter, he found his legs shaking.

Tano pressed the intercom button.

"What?" someone answered gruffly.

"Rosalia, it's me, Tano."

"What do you want?"

"Let me in and I'll tell you."

"You'd better be quick. I haven't got time to waste."

Roberto was surprised by the brusqueness of their interaction and worried for Tano's future romantic life. Would he ever find a wife if he treated girls so gruffly?

The door buzzed open and Roberto followed Tano up a flight of stairs. Rosalia was waiting for them at the door of her flat.

"I'm busy, Tano. I'm going on holiday with my boyfriend. You should have thought about this before." Then she saw Roberto and her expression changed. "Gosh, you've brought the priest with you! You still won't change my mind, you know?"

Roberto was increasingly confused. There seemed to be a subtext to this conversation which he couldn't decipher.

"Let us in," Tano said, stepping towards the door with a brashness Roberto had never seen in him before.

The girl sighed and stepped away from the doorway only enough to let them through.

Inside the flat, two large suitcases lay open on the floor and the whole living room was strewn with swimming suits, sarongs and sunhats.

Roberto, was usually travelled with just one set of spare clothes, concluded that she must be emigrating to a foreign country to sell Signora Albi's jewels and live off the money.

With the confidence of someone feeling quite at home, Tano pushed some swimming suits aside and sat on the couch. Roberto remained standing.

"What is it you want?" the girl asked Tano. "This is really not a good time. I'm going in two hours."

"I know."

"If you wanted to get back together, you should have told me earlier."

Back together? So they had been boyfriend and girlfriend. Tano's familiarity with her made sense now, but Roberto couldn't believe that Tano had held back such important information.

"Don't imagine that I'm going to marry you just because you've brought a priest with you."

She sounded a little upset, and Roberto wondered if marrying Tano had been her wish during their relationship.

Tano swatted the air. "Nah. I don't want to marry you and I don't want to get back together. I just need your help."

At such a callous response, Roberto faith's

in Tano's ability to manage this difficult conversation instantly shattered.

"Are you going somewhere nice?" Roberto hurried to ask, hoping to distract the girl from Tano's insensitive remarks.

"I'm going to the Maldives," she said, flicking her hair back and glancing at Tano to check his reaction.

The Maldives sounded like a place where someone with an unexpected windfall might go, Roberto thought.

"But don't tell anyone," she added quickly, looking over her shoulders.

"Why?" Roberto asked.

She glanced at the door. "Because we've told everyone that we're going to Greece. We don't want anyone to know where we got the money from."

"Where did you get it from?" Roberto asked, hopeful for a confession.

"My boyfriend won the lottery." Chin raised, she glanced at Tano to check his reaction.

Tano scoffed. "I bet the 'lottery' is Ciccio Titotto or Tonio Moneta."

"Even if it was? He has money and can treat me well—unlike you."

Roberto felt that they should leave before Tano and Rosalia hurt each other any further.

The girl was clearly innocent of the disappearance of the ring.

"Thank you for your time," he told her. "We shall let you carry on with your packing now." He turned to Tano to leave but the young man remained seated.

"Rosalia has nothing to pack for," he said. "She's not going anywhere."

"What are you on about?" she asked, fists planted on her hips.

"Signora Albi thinks that you've stolen one of her rings and she's about to go to the police to tell them. They will catch you as soon as you try to get on any plane," Tano said, deadpan.

Roberto had never imagined Tano bluffing like this. He was showing a side of himself that Roberto hadn't known. Maybe he would have made a successful criminal if he had chosen to. Roberto shuddered at the thought.

"But I didn't!" the girl protested.

"That won't stop the police coming for you if Signora thinks you did. You were alone in her room where you said you were collecting her 'dry cleaning'," Tano said, making quote marks in the air. "You cleaned her out all right."

Rosalia looked horrified. "I don't know anything about any ring! I just picked up the dry cleaning she had left on her chair. I didn't touch anything else!"

Roberto felt that she was telling the truth. In which case, Tano's bluff wasn't going to achieve anything other than upsetting the girl. "We believe you," he said.

"No, I don't," Tano said. "She's lying. She took the ring and she's going on holiday with the money."

"Surely it would have taken her more than a day to sell a ring and book a holiday," Roberto pointed out.

Tano folded his arms and harrumphed. "I still think she's guilty."

Rosalia shot a fiery look at Tano. "I'm not!"

"If she didn't do it, then who did it?" Tano asked Roberto in exasperation.

The girl pointed her finger at Tano. "You, of course!"

Rosalia and Tano both turned to Roberto for a verdict.

"It's been neither of you, so you can start making peace," Roberto decreed.

Rosalia glanced at Tano with a glint of satisfaction.

"This means that someone else has got that ring," Roberto continued, "and we've still got to find him or her."

"It's got to be the man who came in after me," Rosalia said.

"What man?" Roberto asked.

Tano slapped his forehead. "How could I have forgotten!"

***

Having reassured Rosalia that Signora Albi had no suspicions about her and that she could go on holiday without fear, they said goodbye.

"It would have been helpful if you had told me earlier about the man fixing the roller blind in Signora's room," Roberto said while Tano unlocked the chain around his scooter.

"I'm sorry. I forgot."

"You also forgot that Rosalia had been your girlfriend."

"She wasn't my girlfriend."

"She seemed to think she was."

"She misunderstood."

Roberto couldn't imagine how such a misunderstanding could arise but decided he didn't want to know the details.

"Do you remember the company's name of the roller blind man?"

"No idea."

"Did you not ask for an identification card?"

"It's not my job to check that the tradesmen Signora calls are properly registered."

"It's not about that. Never mind. If you don't know the name of the company, we'll have to ask Signora."

Tano dropped the chain. "No, don't talk to

Signora!"

"Why?"

Was Tano hiding something from him? After all, he had already withheld important information about Rosalia and the roller blind man. Roberto couldn't imagine Tano stealing the ring, but he could imagine him picking it up to admire it and losing it.

"Is there something else you haven't told me?" Roberto pressed.

"No." Tano looked sheepishly at the ground. "I just don't want her to think about me. If she doesn't think of me, maybe she will forget."

"That's not how it works," Roberto said.

"Anyway, we don't need to ask her for the name of their company. If you want to know it, we can go and ask them ourselves."

"How? We need their name to find them."

"I know where they are."

"Why didn't you tell me?"

"You asked me if I knew their name, not if I knew where they are."

Roberto sighed. He hadn't found even his Philosophy degree course as abstruse as conversations with Tano.

***

It was no wonder Tano didn't know the name of handyman's business. It wasn't printed even on the signage of the shop. In fact, "shop" was a grandiose word for what looked like somebody's garage.

Roberto realised he had been naïve to assume that someone as wealthy as Signora Albi would use more professional-looking contractors. Perhaps this was the way wealthy people stayed so.

One side of the shabby room was stacked with bottled gas for stoves, the other with bottled mineral water, and in between were boxes of candles and matches—everything a poorly connected home could need. Roberto wondered how their repairs business fitted in with their selling business.

Two men, who looked like father and son, were working at a grimy worktop. They stopped what they were doing when Roberto and Tano entered the room.

Roberto felt like he was walking into someone's home rather than a shop, and that he wasn't welcome.

"Good afternoon," he greeted the men.

The older man nodded and waited, presumably for Roberto to explain the reason for his visit.

"Do you repair roller blinds of domestic properties?"

The older man nodded. Roberto wondered

if he was actually able to speak. The younger man picked up a diary and a pen.

"When?" the younger man asked.

"I'd like to see your work first. Have you done any roller blind repairs recently?"

The two men looked at each other in confusion at the unusual request.

"Yes, we have," the dad replied.

"Signora Albi's?" the son asked the dad.

The dad shook his head and shot the son a reproachful glance, then turned to Roberto. "You can check out number seven on this road, first floor."

"Did you just say you've done Signora Albi's roller blinds too?" Roberto asked, hopeful for more information.

Did the father not want it mentioned because they hadn't done a good job or was there a more serious reason?

"You've heard wrong. Check out number seven and come back if you want us to do yours," the dad said conclusively. "You won't find anyone doing the job as well and as cheaply as we do."

Roberto thanked them and left with Tano.

"I don't think he recognised me, but I recognised the younger guy. He's the one who repaired Signora Albi's blind," Tano whispered.

"But for some reason they don't want us to know about it," Roberto mused. "Asking them again would be pointless and would only make them suspicious about us. I'm not sure what to do."

"We must search their shop," Tano suggested.

"How? They don't seem to be going anywhere and they're surely not going to leave it unlocked overnight," Roberto said, looking at the large padlocks for the metal shutters.

Just then, the shutters of a ground floor window opened cautiously, and an old woman beckoned them with a finger.

Roberto and Tano walked up to her.

The woman glanced up and down the street, then whispered, "A word of advice. Don't have any work done by those cowboys."

"What's wrong with them?" Roberto asked.

"They're dishonest. They do a poor job and take a lot of money."

"I see. Thank you," Roberto replied with a hint of disappointment.

He had hoped for information that might lead them to the ring.

"That's not all," the woman continued.

"Really?"

"I bet they didn't look pleased to have visitors when you walked into the shop, am I right?"

"Yes."

"That's not normal, is it? Shopkeepers should be pleased to see customers, shouldn't they?"

Roberto nodded and wished she would come to the point.

"Well, there's a reason. I can see their back garden from my upstairs windows and I can tell you why."

Roberto realised she expected him to ask why. "Why?"

"In that back garden of theirs, they keep stuff that shouldn't be there." She pursed her lips and grabbed the shutters to close them. This was the end of her story.

"Wait! What stuff?" Roberto asked.

The woman glanced up and down the street. "They don't live just off selling bottled gas and doing odd jobs, that's all I'm saying." She tapped the side of her nose to mean that she had shared confidential information and closed the shutters.

Roberto looked at Tano. "If these guys are dishonest, there are good chances that the young man has taken the ring just because he had the opportunity."

"We need to find out what they keep in their back garden," Tano said.

"How?"

"I've got a crowbar at home," Tano suggested hopefully.

"No way. We're not breaking and entering. That would put us on the wrong side of the law."

"I thought we were already there."

"Not yet. So we mustn't make a mistake which will land us in deeper trouble."

Tano sighed. "Okay. What's the plan then?"

"That tree overhangs the back of the men's shop. If we climb on it, we should be able to see their garden and possibly inside the back of the shop," Roberto suggested.

Tano took a step back. "No way! I'm not climbing trees. It's what children do, and I won't be seen doing that."

Roberto glanced up and down the deserted alley. "By who?"

"Girls."

"It's just past lunchtime, it's very hot, and everyone is resting at home in the shade."

"I don't care. You climb the tree while I distract the men in the shop."

The tree was only a slender ailanthus but Roberto was the human equivalent to it, so he judged that the tree could take his weight.

He set his sight on a branch that would allow him a good view and started climbing. But when he got on it, he discovered that a sunshade blocked the view. Fortunately, the wall met the tree at that point. Would it count as trespassing if he stepped on the wall?

It certainly would be a pity to give up now that he was so close. Roberto stepped onto the wall.

Now he had a good view of the back garden. It was littered with old furniture, a rusting motorbike and the kind of vehicle parts that could easily be stolen from parked cars and scooters. This must be what the woman was talking about.

But if they had stolen the ring, they certainly wouldn't be keeping it in the back garden.

The door into the back of the shop was wide open but a fly curtain blocked Roberto's view. Every now and then, the breeze moved the beaded strings, but the darkness indoors made it impossible to see inside.

Roberto shuffled along the wall to get a better view. When the breeze parted the curtain again, he glimpsed a simple bed and a table inside. So this must be the men's home.

Roberto had assumed that the back of the shop would be a storeroom brimming with stock—hard to search for a small ring. But if it was a simple home with little furniture and few possessions, it shouldn't take much to search it, Roberto thought.

He estimated the distance from the wall to the ground. He should be able to lower himself down without damage to himself or to others' possessions.

As he slithered down the dusty white wall, he discovered that black clergy clothes were not ideal for this job—which was as well, because sneaking into other people's homes wasn't a job for a priest. What was he doing there? he thought with a shudder as his feet touched the patio's tiles. If he got caught, he would bring shame on the Catholic Church and make his and Tano's situation a lot worse.

But he was already so close to that fly curtain that he might as well finish the job and, hopefully, recover the ring.

Roberto waited for the next breath of breeze to jangle the fly curtain to part it and tiptoe through.

When his eyes had adjusted from the brightness outside, he found himself in a room with two beds, a simple wardrobe and a table with two chairs. A small kitchen took up one wall, and the other wall had two closed doors. There were no ornaments, no pictures, nothing that had no practical function.

Roberto searched the wardrobe, under the beds, the kitchen cupboards and drawers. No ring. He looked under the beds and checked for loose tiles that might hide secret compartments. Nothing.

The next to search was the bathroom, which must be one of the two doors. But which one? If he opened the wrong one, he would probably step into the front of the shop and find himself face-to-face with the men.

He listened carefully for Tano's voice. Amazingly, the young man had managed to engage the men and a passionate conversation was going on over the virtues and faults of various players in the Palermo football team.

Roberto was sure that the voices were coming from the door on the left. So he opened the door on the right.

A crack was all he needed to see the side of a gas bottle and a foot hitched on the wooden bar of a stool.

This was it—he was done for, he thought, as his heart jumped into his throat.

But the man pushed the door closed with his foot. "Damn wind," he muttered.

Roberto had to steady himself against the wall, he was so dizzy with fear. He'd been lucky this time, but there was no room for more mistakes.

He opened the other door carefully. Yes, it was a bathroom, and not a very clean one.

Roberto opened the rickety cabinet. There were rolls of cannabis and bags of unlabelled powders and tablets. If this was the men's stash of illegal items, the stolen ring should be there, but it wasn't.

Maybe the two men didn't have the ring after all. It wouldn't have made any sense to steal a ring and attract the attention of the police when they had so much more to hide. Roberto realised with dismay that he had risked his and Tano's reputation for nothing. He had better leave before he got caught and had no ring to justify himself.

Squeezing through the fly curtain again, he tiptoed out into garden. Roberto now realised that the garden wall was completely smooth. This had been great when he was sliding down it, but it was a problem now that he wanted to climb it. He needed a foothold.

An abandoned couch looked like just the thing. Roberto stepped on the armrest, then on the backrest. But as he did so, the back cracked and his leg went through the wood and foam, tearing his trousers.

Thankfully, he wasn't hurt. He stepped back on the armrest and, with a lot of effort and undignified scrambling, he managed to get up on the wall and back on the tree.

Everything seemed to be difficult in this

direction and climbing down the tree, too, turned out to be more difficult than climbing up. Roberto was almost down when he heard a familiar voice.

"Zaccheus, come down from that tree!"

It was Corrado, quoting the episode in the Gospel when Jesus meets a notorious sinner who's climbed a tree to see him. In this case, Corrado would be the equivalent of Jesus and Roberto the notorious sinner.

Roberto jumped. Corrado was the last person he wanted to be seen by at this moment.

"Have you lost a football in someone else's garden?"

"Please, be quiet," Roberto begged, jumping off the tree and landing unsteadily on his feet.

"You've always been hopeless at climbing trees," Corrado said, apparently unable to whisper. He gave Roberto a once over. "Look at the state of you. What mischief have you been up to?"

"Please, keep your voice down. I'll explain when we get home," Roberto pleaded.

"Who are you afraid of?"

Corrado clearly wasn't going to let go until his curiosity was satisfied.

"The people in this shop," Roberto whispered.

"I know them."

"How?"

"The son has come to the church with his fiancée to set a date for their wedding."

"Has he just got engaged?" Roberto asked, immediately thinking about the ring again.

"I would imagine so."

Signora Albi had told Roberto that her ring was an engagement ring. Could it be a coincidence that it had disappeared just after a man in need of one had come into her house? Perhaps Roberto hadn't found the ring in the man's home because he had already given it to his fiancée!

"Thank you, brother! You've just solved the mystery!"

***

Finding out who the bride-to-be was had been easy. Amanda Peluso's details were in the weddings booking diary in the parish office. Breaking the news that her engagement ring wasn't hers to keep was going to be harder.

Roberto had prepared what he was going to say and had played the scene out in his mind. As Tano had never seen the ring, Roberto asked Signora Albi to come along to identify it.

She wasn't keen at all but she agreed to meet them at the perfume shop where Amanda Peluso worked.

"I can't wait to see Signora Albi's face when

she sees the ring on the girl's finger," Tano told Roberto as they waited for Signora Albi outside the shop. "She's going to be so sorry for accusing me unfairly. Do you think that she'll go down on her knees to beg me to forgive her?"

"I wouldn't raise my hopes too much, Tano. Just concentrate on getting your job back."

"I'm never going back to her."

"Don't take any rash decision. Feelings are running high at the moment, but in future you might regret not having this job experience under your belt."

Tano nodded. "You're right. You're always wise. That's why they've made you a priest."

"That's not quite how it works…" Roberto said, then stopped. "There, Signora is coming."

Signora Alba didn't look like she was about to beg anyone for forgiveness anytime soon.

"I won't be pleased if you've called me here for nothing," she told them as a greeting.

"We haven't. You'll find your ring on the finger of the woman who works in this shop," Tano declared, filling his chest defiantly.

"We'll see, young man."

They stepped into the shop and a young woman stood up from her chair behind a counter.

"Good morning. How can I help you?" she

asked them politely.

Roberto had hoped to see her hands as soon as they walked in, but the girl was keeping her hands in her apron's pockets. This required plan B.

"We'd like to buy a gift for a man," Roberto said.

"How about an aftershave?"

"Good idea."

The girl turned to the display cabinet and finally extracted her hands from her pockets.

"That's not my ring!" Signora Albi cried out.

The girl whipped round with a frightened expression.

"The ring on her finger isn't mine!" Signora Albi repeated angrily to Roberto, as if he might have misunderstood her the first time. "You've given me false hopes and wasted my time. You'll have to do a lot better than this if you don't want me to turn you in to the police!"

With that, she stormed out of the shop.

"What's the matter with her?" the girl asked Roberto.

Roberto sighed. "It's a long story."

"Has she got a problem with my engagement ring? Because my fiancée bought it for me. We chose it together," she said proudly.

"Don't worry about it. It was just a

misunderstanding."

Roberto felt that, after all this trouble, he should at least buy an aftershave from the girl, even if he didn't use any. So he did.

When they regrouped outside the shop, Tano held his head in his hands in exasperation. "If she hasn't got it, then where is that blasted ring?"

"The man could have stolen it and sold it to buy a new one so that he wouldn't raise any suspicions."

"To buy that ring on the girl's finger? He must have got a very bad deal, poor guy. I'm sure Signora Albi's ring was worth a lot more than that," Tano said.

Roberto was glad he was never going to buy an engagement ring for a woman, if this was the sort of scrutiny a man would get.

"Perhaps he's kept some of the money back to pay for the wedding party. In any case we should check all the second-hand jewellers," Roberto decided.

Tano sucked air. "So long as I'm not the one asking Signora Albi for a photo of the ring."

***

At first, Signora Albi told Roberto that he should ask Tano what the ring looked like, as the young man had surely stolen it and was taking Roberto for a ride. Eventually, though,

Roberto persuaded her to give him a photo anyway.

It was a distinctive ring in the Art Deco style, including a large pearl as well as two big diamonds. It wouldn't be difficult to recognise.

Armed with the photo, Roberto and Tano visited all the second-hand jewellers nearby but none of them had seen a ring like that. Then Roberto and Tano tried the jewellers in posher parts of the city and found a couple of rings which were a little similar, but none of them was the one.

All this time, Signora Albi kept phoning Roberto to ask him for updates and to repeat that "that boy" was taking him for a ride.

"The only ride he is taking me on is on his scooter," Roberto told Signora firmly.

He didn't explain, though, that this was unpleasant enough.

At one point, Tano's scooter ran out of fuel and they had to push it to a petrol station. Roberto tried to pay for the fuel but Tano refused.

Roberto felt it wasn't fair that Tano should be wasting his money and time to clear his name of a crime he hadn't done. If he hadn't put him forward for that job, Roberto thought with regret, Tano wouldn't have found himself in this situation.

On Saturday evening, when the last jeweller shop closed for the weekend, Roberto and Tano were no closer to finding the ring than they had been when Signora Albi had given her ultimatum.

Tomorrow Signora Albi would be reporting the theft to the police and Tano would automatically become the main suspect. Had Tano kept on the straight and narrow for all these years, only to end up in prison and be treated like a criminal anyway?

***

The church was already closed when Roberto was dropped off home.

At least he hadn't had to worry about his parish duties over these days, thanks to Corrado. Today his brother had celebrated the dawn Mass, had taken a funeral in the mid-morning, had taught the children's catechism class in the afternoon and, finally, had given a talk at the marriage preparation course in the evening.

This last one was a particularly welcome swap because Roberto hadn't enjoyed his first session with that group, and hadn't been looking forward to the next.

"How did the marriage preparation session go?" he asked his brother when they were having supper with Father Pietro.

"Very successful, indeed. I received several compliments for my talk on marriage in the Bible."

Roberto tried not to feel jealous. Of course his brother would give better talks than he could. Corrado was a scholar who spent his days studying and poring over books. He didn't spend his time arranging jobs for parishioners, and he certainly didn't chase after runaway rings.

"Was anybody late to the session?" Roberto probed.

"No. Everyone was there early and fully… engaged." Corrado smiled at his own pun.

Roberto tried to suppress a prick of disappointment. Even Giovanni and Clara behaved well for Corrado. Why couldn't he have some of his brother's touch?

"And how did Mass go?" Roberto asked, wondering if his brother had managed to sing.

"Very well. I taught your congregation some new hymns, which they sang with gusto."

"Your brother's stay has been a great pleasure," Father Pietro put in. "I'm just sorry that it's come at a great cost to him."

"Don't even mention it," Corrado said.

"What great cost?" Roberto asked, confused.

Corrado's train ticket hadn't been unusually

expensive, and Roberto intended to refund him as soon as he could.

"Nothing important," Corrado replied, waving a dismissive hand.

"Actually, it is quite important," Father Pietro contradicted him, and turned to Roberto. "I'm surprised he hasn't told you. Your brother was expecting a visit from a bishop about the work he's doing at the Observatory. Yesterday, the bishop finally came and Corrado wasn't there."

"Oh no, I'm sorry."

"It's okay. I missed parish life and I welcomed a little reminder," Corrado said kindly, before warning, "but I've done it now and I won't need reminding again for a very long time!"

***

Sunday had arrived but they still hadn't found the ring or any information that could help find it.

Now that Corrado had gone home, Roberto had to return to his parish duties and celebrate the first Sunday morning Mass. At the end of the service, he met Agostino and Maria.

"We missed you at the last session," they told him.

"I hear the session went very well," Roberto said, trying to push any envy out of his heart.

Agostino and Maria glanced at each other. "We wouldn't exactly say that. Your brother is probably more used to talking to scholars, and some of his lecture was way above our heads. But it was obvious that he was trying his best."

"He told me that all the couples were on time."

"Only because Giovanni and Clara didn't even turn up," Maria said. "In fact, Agostino and I wanted to have a word with you about them."

"We suspect that they don't want to get married," Agostino explained. "Skipping sessions, arriving late and being disengaged might just be acts of rebellion against their wedding."

"But they'll go through with it if we don't stop them," Maria said.

"Why would they get married against their will?" Roberto asked.

"Their families must be putting pressure on them. This marriage would cement an alliance between the two main criminal families of our neighbourhood."

"We can't let this wedding go ahead. I'll inform Father Pietro and we'll talk to Giovanni and Clara and their families. If they insist on going ahead with the wedding, they'll have to get married somewhere else."

Roberto looked forward to talking to the two criminal families as little as he looked forward to his meeting with Signora Albi.

Unfortunately, it was time to go.

Tano was already waiting for Roberto outside on his scooter. "I've changed my mind. I'll just drop you off. I don't want to see Signora Albi," he told Roberto.

"That's a bad idea. Signora Albi will take it as proof of your guilt."

Tano sighed. "Okay."

They rode in silence—Tano without his helmet, because he didn't see the point in wearing it if he was going to jail anyway.

When they got to the villa, Signora Albi was waiting for them at the top of the steps.

"Have you got my ring?" she asked in the place of a greeting.

"No, but—"

"Then there's no need for you to come inside," Signora interrupted. "I have nothing more to say to you or to hear from you, and I don't want anything else to disappear from my house." She glanced pointedly at Tano.

"It wasn't me! You can't accuse me without proof!" Tano shouted.

Roberto instantly regretted bringing him along.

Signora Albi's nostrils flared. "The ring

you've stolen from me was only money to you, but to me it was a lot more! My son was going to propose to his girlfriend today, but now he can't. He and Arianna live in Rome and it's been very hard to arrange their visit. But now it's been for nothing."

Signora Albi looked very upset and Roberto felt for her. Then a thought struck him.

"Did you just say that it's been hard to arrange this visit?"

"Yes. We struggled to find a date when Arianna was able to come."

"But she's here now?"

"Yes. They've both been here for a few days now. But there will be no engagement!"

"May I speak to Arianna?"

"If you're thinking of apologising to her, absolutely not. She has no idea that Filippo was going to propose."

Roberto wasn't so sure about that. And this might be the key to solving the mystery of the runaway ring.

"I promise that I won't spoil any surprises."

Reluctantly, Signora Albi let them into the house. She escorted them to the sitting room and, unwilling to leave them alone, she rang Arianna on her phone and asked her to come down.

Roberto and Tano sat on the sofa while

Signora Albi stood over them like a guard.

Tano ran a finger over the coffee table. "Your new housekeeper isn't doing as good a job as me."

"I haven't hired one yet. Once burned, twice shy."

She stared hard at him and he frowned back. Roberto's hopes that Tano would ever get his job back were vaporised.

"Tano, you told me that, on the morning the ring disappeared, there was nobody else in the house except you and the family. Did you include Arianna in the family?"

"Yes. It was me, Arianna and Signor Albi at home."

A young woman walked into the room, saw Roberto and Tano and frowned a little.

"Hello Arianna. This is Father Roberto. He asked to meet you."

"Hello," Roberto greeted her, and made space for her to sit between him and Tano, but Arianna remained standing.

"Hi."

"You are Filippo's girlfriend, am I right?" Roberto asked.

"Yes?" The hint of question in her voice was meant to encourage Roberto to carry on, but it sounded like she was unsure about her answer.

"I would like to tell a story," Roberto said.

"I hope you're not wasting our time," Signora Albi interrupted.

"I'm not. It's relevant. Once upon a time, a young man and a young woman were much in love with each other. He wanted to marry her but she wasn't sure about it. Maybe she had seen other marriages fail, or she feared for her career, or she just didn't feel ready yet."

Arianna took a small step back. "I don't see why you're telling me this story."

But Roberto continued. "When the young woman sensed that he was about to propose, she panicked. She didn't want to say yes, but she was afraid she'd lose him if she rejected his proposal. So she did the only thing she could think that would to stop him proposing." Roberto looked intensely at Arianna. "Perhaps you'd like to continue the story?"

"I didn't know what else to do," she said, trembling.

Signora Albi looked from one to the other in confusion. "I don't understand."

"I took your ring, Petronia," Arianna said. "I was going to put it back in your jewellery box just before I left."

Signora Petronia still looked baffled. "Why would you do that?"

"Just like the priest said, I didn't want Filippo to propose. I heard him talking to you on the phone about it and I panicked. I'm not ready for thinking about marriage yet. I just want everything to remain the same for a little longer. But, I guess, now I've ruined it all anyway."

She slumped into the nearest chair and burst into tears.

Signora Albi hugged her. "I'm sorry, it's all been my fault. I put pressure on Filippo to propose."

Roberto got up and signalled to Tano that it was time to go and leave them alone.

"She hasn't said sorry to me yet," Tano said loudly.

"She will do it another time. Let's go now," Roberto whispered.

As they rode home, Tano asked Roberto how he knew that Arianna had taken the ring.

"When Signora Albi said that it had been hard to get Arianna to visit them, I remembered a couple at our parish's marriage preparation course. It's been very hard to get them to attend the classes, and that's because neither of them actually wants to get married."

Roberto was careful to omit their names and respect their privacy.

"Ah, yes. Giovanni and Clara," Tano said carelessly.

"How did you know?"

"Everyone in the neighbourhood knows that they don't want to get married, and hopes that you and Father Pietro will stop it happening."

"That's very kind."

"Nah, we don't give a fig about them. They're as nasty as each other. We just don't want their families to join forces."

"I see. But why has nobody told Father Pietro or me?"

"Giovanni and Clara couldn't tell you because their families would be very angry if they found out. And everyone else thought you knew and you didn't want to make a fuss because you were afraid."

"That's not true! I might not be brave but Father Pietro certainly is," Roberto protested.

"Don't put yourself down, Father. You're brave too."

As the scooter sped past a car on the wrong side of the road, Roberto thought that Tano was probably right.

***

Later that evening, Roberto was collecting the laundry from the roof terrace when his phone rang. He immediately recognised his mistake in taking his phone with him to the only place where he was guaranteed solitude. Too late now.

To Roberto's surprise, it was Corrado.

"I just wanted to let you know that I've arrived safely," his brother announced. "In case you were wondering."

Roberto hadn't been wondering at all—any train would be a million times safer than Tano's scooter—and he felt a little guilty. "Great. Thank you for letting me know."

"How is it going with that matter of a stolen ring?"

Ah, this was the real reason for the call, Roberto thought. "All solved. The culprit has confessed, Signora Albi has apologised and has offered Tano his job back, which he has accepted."

"Lucky the culprit came forward!" Corrado said.

Roberto was about to explain that the culprit wouldn't have come forward if he hadn't pieced the mystery together, but he decided to leave it. Pride was a sin.

"Quite."

"By the way, thank you for the aftershave," Corrado said.

As Roberto didn't use aftershave, he had gifted the one he had bought at the perfume shop to Corrado. He imagined his brother wearing it and was touched.

"It's my pleasure. I wasn't sure if you used

aftershave," Roberto said.

"Actually, I don't. But I've given it to the bishop who came to discuss my research and didn't find me. It seems to have earned me his forgiveness."

Roberto smiled. It was fair enough that his brother should regift it to make amends for the trouble caused by his absence.

"When are you going to visit me?" Corrado asked unexpectedly. "You've never done it."

Roberto was about to point out that he had never been invited but he wondered if, behind his reproaching tone, Corrado might be trying to be genuinely nice.

"I'd love to visit you," he said instead.

"I'll be waiting for you."

They hung up and Roberto looked out of the terrace at the sun setting behind the mountains. It painted the sky the colours of apricots and peaches. Roberto felt that no dome in the Vatican could be more beautiful than the sky of his beloved Sicily. But he would still make the effort to visit Corrado.

His brother's attitude could be infuriating, but his actions had shown that he cared about Roberto. Without Corrado's help, Roberto couldn't have devoted his time to solving the mystery of the missing ring.

Roberto thought about how close he had

been to giving up. If it hadn't been for the recalcitrant couple at the marriage preparation classes, Roberto wouldn't have thought of an act of self-sabotage like Arianna's. There seemed to be a thousand different ways in which romantic love could bring heartache — even when fully requited. Roberto was glad to be safely outside that realm.

But it wasn't just romantic love that had its complications and upsets. Roberto had felt miserable when his young friend had been in danger of ending up in prison. Youth was too short to be wasted in a cell, and Roberto had always been sure of Tano's innocence. But now Tano had a job—with the income, purpose and dignity that came with it—and Roberto was very happy about it.

Now he could go back to his job too—that of looking after all the other sheep of the fold, not just the black one. One of the tasks on his list was to improve the screening of couples entering the marriage preparation course.
But right now, alone and undisturbed on the roof terrace, he could enjoy the cupolas of the cathedral, the honey-coloured bell tower and the cobalt sea in the distance, and feel happy with himself and the world.

2. THE ELOPERS' ESCAPADE

Father Roberto loved praying in the church at night. Then, when all his parishioners were tucked in bed in their homes and the church's big wooden doors were closed, he could enjoy God's company without interruptions.

Kneeling in the front pew and watching the tremulous flame of the candle, he thought of young Samuel in the Bible called by God while he slept in the sanctuary.

Roberto was just imagining how lovely it must be to hear God's call, when a loud knock rattled the church doors. Roberto jumped. Was this God's call for him?

He rushed to the door where he heard two—very human—voices.

"Let us in! We need your help!" a man and a woman pleaded.

Roberto had barely unlocked the heavy doors when a young couple slipped into the church.

"Quick, Father, lock the doors again!" the young man urged.

Roberto complied. "What's the matter?" he asked.

"We need you to marry us right now," the young woman said. "I'm Loretta and this is my fiancée, Matteo."

"It's bedtime. Why such a hurry?"

"Our families don't want us to get married," Matteo said.

"I'm sure that some kind of agreement can be reached with dialogue and patience."

"No, Father. Our families are connected with Tonio Moneta and Ciccio Titotto. They don't solve problems with dialogue and patience. They do it with guns," Loretta explained.

Roberto recognised the names of the two rival criminal bosses of the neighbourhood. This was a dangerous matter and he mustn't try to deal with it on his own.

"I'll talk to the parish priest, Father Pietro," he reassured the couple. "You'd better go home now before you're seen together and get into trouble."

"You can't send us away. We might have

already been seen coming here together," Matteo pointed out.

"We're your responsibility now," Loretta added with a smile.

"We've got our documents with us. Please, marry us," Matteo pleaded

"I'm sorry but it's not an instant thing. At the very least, we need to publish the marriage banns and keep them up on the noticeboard for at least eight days. Then you need a number of certificates, wedding witnesses and that's even without considering the marriage preparation classes…"

"Okay. Then, while you get all that done for us, we wait here, under God's protection," Loretta said, pointing to the large crucifix above the altar, "and yours."

***

Roberto gave up any hope of continuing his prayers. God had indeed called him—as loudly and clearly as the young couple's knocks on the church's doors.

Father Pietro must be fast asleep at this hour, Roberto thought as he climbed the stairs up to the presbytery. How was he going to wake him without scaring him out of his skin?

Roberto turned on the corridor light and opened the door of Father Pietro's bedroom just enough to let some light in. And immediately saw that something was wrong.

The bed was empty.

Roberto threw the door wide open and turned on the overhead light. Father Pietro's bed was unmade, his drawers were open and rummaged through, and his possessions were scattered on the floor.

"Thieves!" Roberto cried indignantly.

"No. I'd say kidnappers." Matteo's voice came from behind Roberto.

The troublesome couple had followed him.

"What are you doing up here?" Roberto asked.

"We thought we'd check out where we're staying," Matteo replied calmly.

"You're not staying here. This is the priests' home."

"Where are we staying then?" Loretta asked.

Roberto couldn't think of any suitable accommodation other than the presbytery's spare room for one of them and the sofa for the other, given that they were not yet married. The situation was getting very complicated very quickly.

"Never mind for now," Roberto snapped. "First of all, I need to find Father Pietro."

"You won't find him. They must have taken him away," Loretta said.

Roberto felt a swell of panic. "Who has

taken him? Why?"

How was could he possibly deal with this double crisis without his mentor and friend?

"Does Father Pietro own a suitcase? I'm sure you'll find that it's missing," Matteo said.

Roberto searched the room. Yes, Father Pietro's little backpack was missing.

"What does it mean?"

"That the kidnappers allowed him to pack a few items to take along," Loretta explained. "So the mess you see around is not caused by thieves but by Father Pietro packing in a hurry."

"How long are these people intending to keep him for?" Roberto asked in dismay.

"However long it takes to stop us getting married, I suppose," Loretta replied. "It's a good sign that he was allowed to pack. It means he's going to be treated well."

Roberto couldn't imagine there being anything good in the situation at all.

"Although, by the looks of things, he's not taken very much," Matteo commented.

He was right. Just like Jesus had sent his disciples out to preach with nothing but a staff and a pair of sandals, Father Pietro seemed to have taken the bare minimum. One big difference, Roberto thought with a stab of sadness, was that the disciples had been sent in

pairs while Father Pietro was all alone and
Roberto, who should have gone with him, had
been left behind.

"Who has kidnapped him?" Roberto asked
indignantly.

"Our families, of course—to stop our
wedding."

Roberto felt a swell of antipathy towards the
couple who were causing him and his beloved
mentor so much trouble.

"Then why didn't they take me too?" he
asked stroppily.

"Because they knew you wouldn't do
anything without Father Pietro's permission."

"Time to call the police then."

"No!" the couple cried out in unison.

"You would get our families into trouble."

"I imagine that wouldn't be anything new,"
he retorted crabbily.

"Please, don't," they begged.

"Anyway, only one of your families will be
in trouble—whichever one has taken Father
Pietro."

Roberto looked from one to the other
questioningly and the two looked at each other.

"We have no idea which one has done it."

"Let's look for a note or any clue," Matteo
suggested.

Father Pietro had few possessions and it

didn't take long to search the small room. No note or any other clue had been left behind. Roberto sighed.

"Don't worry, Father. You're not alone. You've got us and we can help you," Loretta reassured him.

"We know where our families keep unwilling guests," Matteo explained.

"Do they regularly take 'unwilling guests'?" Roberto asked, aghast.

"Only when necessary."

"My job is to bring them food and make sure they're well and comfortable, so I know the place very well," Loretta said proudly.

"Loretta and I shouldn't leave the sanctuary of the church, but as you're not going to marry us without Father Pietro's consent, we have no choice but go looking for him with you," Matteo said magnanimously.

Loretta smiled. "Aren't you lucky to have us?"

Roberto bit his tongue.

***

"Have you got a car?" Matteo asked Roberto.

"No. I don't drive. Can't we get there on foot?"

"No. Both hideouts are in the countryside," they told him.

Roberto felt a pang of sadness imagining Father Pietro held prisoner in some rickety hut in the depths of the Sicilian mountains.

"But there's Father Pietro's car—if either of you can drive it."

Loretta volunteered to drive and Roberto took a packet of biscuits and a flask of water for Father Pietro.

As they left the city behind, the road cut across olive groves and forests of maritime pine and holly oak. Once Roberto's eyes had adjusted to the lack of streetlights, he admired the moon shining full and bright on the hills on one side, and the shore on the other. The sea glittered with silver and gold sequins of moonlight and night-fishing boats.

What a beautiful island, he thought. It would be a garden of Eden if it weren't for some of its worst inhabitants. He thought of Father Pietro, snatched from his bed by thugs, and his heart squeezed. He should have been upstairs by Father Pietro's side, not down in the church, blissfully enjoying his prayers.

Unfortunately, Roberto reflected, he, like all humans, had no power over the past—or the future, really. But for God there was no past, present or future, Roberto thought with a warm hope. So Roberto prayed for the past— that Father Pietro might not have been frightened or hurt when the thugs came—and put his prayer in the hands of God, who sees all time at once.

They had reached some steep hills and Loretta screeched up the hairpin bends so fast that Roberto felt sick. He was sure that Father Pietro's car had never been driven so sportily.

At the top of the hill, she turned off the main road onto a dirt track, still without slowing down. The car bounced wildly.

When they finally slowed down and stopped behind a rocky outcrop, Roberto was relieved.

"I'm sorry but we'll have to walk the rest of the way or the sentry might see us," she apologised.

Roberto was more than happy to leave the car and walk.

They walked between the scotch broom, diss grass and prickly pear, then Loretta made a sign to stop.

"From here on, we'll have to be more careful. I'll go ahead and check the position of the sentry," she said, and left Roberto and Matteo hiding behind a large holly oak.

"She's so brave, isn't she?" Matteo said in a lovestruck tone. "I knew she was the one as soon as I met her. Just like that. Has it ever happened to you, Father?"

Roberto assumed it was a rhetorical

question, but then realised that Matteo was waiting for an answer. "No."

"I couldn't tell anyone, of course. My friends and family would have killed me if they found out," Matteo went on.

Roberto wondered if the "killing" wasn't metaphorical.

"I'm not a brave man, Father."

"Neither am I. In fact, I'm not enjoying this at all."

"This is nothing compared to what men in my family are expected to do. You can't imagine."

"I don't think I want to."

"Thankfully my family know my character so they've made me study and I only do their accounts."

"But you're still part of a criminal business. With your skills and qualifications you could make an honest living on your own. Then you could marry Loretta without having to hide."

"It's not so simple, Father. No one can leave the business without leaving the family. They're my family, and the only world I've ever known."

Roberto felt sorry for him. What would he have done if he had been born in that situation?

Loretta returned.

"I can't see any watchmen but that doesn't

mean that there aren't any, hiding. We'll have to be even more careful," she told them.

Roberto quickly discovered that "even more careful" meant army crawling. Despite trying to avoid brambles, nettles and prickly pears, Roberto was pricked and stung, scraped his elbows and tore his trousers' knees.

Eventually they reached a small stone shack.

"My grandfather was a shepherd and he used to stay here in the summer with the flock," Loretta explained. "Then Tonio Moneta approached him and asked him to hide loot and hostages for him, and he agreed. That's how my family started working for Tonio."

Roberto imagined that her ancestor wouldn't have had much freedom to refuse.

They reached the back of the construction.

"There's a loose stone in the wall. If we can get there and dislodge the stone without being seen, we'll be able to peep inside and check if Father Pietro is there," Loretta said.

Unfortunately the loose stone was right by a patch of stinging nettles. As Roberto slithered on his elbows, he wished he had been wearing thicker clothes.

Loretta jiggled a stone out of the wall and put her eye to the gap.

"I can't see anything. Either there's no one

inside or they are staying in the dark," she said.

The thought of Father Pietro kept in a dark hut made Roberto's heart squeeze. He couldn't wait a moment longer to release his friend and mentor.

"Then we must go in now!" he told them.

"Wait! It could be dangerous!" Matteo and Loretta whispered.

But Roberto was already standing up and heading for the door. He flung it open.

"Pietro, don't be afraid! We're here!" he cried out.

The reply was silence.

Moonlight streaming through the door showed a bed, a bucket and a table and chair, but no people.

"I thought you said you weren't brave," Matteo said.

"That wasn't brave. That was irresponsible!" Loretta reproached him. "There could have been armed guards."

"I'm sorry," Roberto apologised.

Roberto was relieved that his friend hadn't been kept in a dark hut. But if he wasn't there, where was he?

"My family has no other hiding places," Loretta said.

"Then, I'm afraid Father Pietro must be with my family," Matteo said.

"What's there to be afraid of?" Roberto asked, a little worried.

"Unfortunately, my family's residence for unwilling guests is not as luxurious."

Roberto's stomach sank.

***

This time Matteo knew the way, so he got behind the wheel of Father Pietro's car. This proved to be a bad choice as he drove even faster than Loretta.

Roberto, who had taken the rear seat, decided that closing his eyes and trying to sleep would be the least frightening or sickening way to travel.

He must have fallen asleep because, next he knew, he woke up to Loretta tapping him on the shoulder.

"Father, you've got to get out of the car. We've got a flat tyre," she told him gently.

Father Pietro had never had a puncture. He was going to be so upset, Roberto thought before he remembered that his friend currently had bigger reasons to be upset.

"If you change the tyre, Father, I'll walk ahead on a recce," Matteo suggested.

"I've no idea how to change a tyre," Roberto replied.

"Then you should teach him," Loretta said to Matteo.

"Why? He doesn't drive," Matteo objected.

"All men should know how to change a tyre," Loretta insisted. "Even if he's a priest, he's still a man."

"Let's just change this tyre," Roberto interrupted, wishing to stop this embarrassing conversation.

Loretta insisted that Roberto should have a go at unscrewing the wheel nuts. But when Roberto took ten minutes on the first nut, she changed her mind and said that Roberto would learn just as well by watching.

Matteo finished the job quickly, turned the car around so that it was ready for a quick getaway, and the three of them set off on foot.

Roberto was glad that this time they didn't need to army-crawl.

The landscape was barren in a way that reminded Roberto of the surface of the moon. A nasty smell filled the air. Roberto hoped that wasn't the smell of corpses.

"Here we are," Matteo said, "my family's disused sulphur mines."

That explained the smell! Phew.

As they stepped through a doorway in the rock, Roberto thought that Matteo hadn't exaggerated when he said that this place would be less luxurious than the shepherd's hut.

"These mines have been in my family for

generations. When the sulphur ran out, my grandfather fell into financial difficulties and turned to Ciccio Titotto for help, and we've been indebted to him ever since."

Lighting the way with their phones' torches, they descended some steep steps and crossed several long and dark corridors held up by rickety wooden beams.

The place wouldn't have been terribly safe when it was still in operation and Roberto couldn't imagine it being any safer now.

Matteo stopped in front of a door which looked a lot newer than the rest of the mine. He turned to Roberto. "Behind this door and the next few ones there could be armed guards, so may I ask you to refrain from any kamikaze initiative, Father?"

A little embarrassed, Roberto nodded.

Matteo performed a distinctive sequence of knocks—a rhythm in between *La Cucaracha* and *Clementine*—then pulled a key out of his pocket and thrust it into the lock.

"Why did you knock if you have a key?" Roberto asked.

"So that they won't shoot us when we open."

Roberto wondered why anyone would shoot someone with a key but perhaps criminals needed to be more careful than ordinary people.

There was nobody on the other side of the door—just an empty corridor with cigarette butts on the ground.

"Strange. They usually guard this door. Perhaps they've decided that Father Pietro is a low-risk guest," Matteo commented.

Roberto imagined Father Pietro praying in his prison like a monk in a cell or a hermit in a hermitage.

The corridor ended with another door. Matteo performed another sequence of knocks—this time, to the rhythm of *Besame Mucho*— and again there was no reply. Matteo unlocked it and they found nobody on the other side.

"Mm…they're really letting standards drop."

The next corridor led to a bigger door.

"This is the last one. There will definitely be someone guarding this."

Matteo knocked *Oh Susanna* on the door, and explained, "The woman who guards the guests is called Susanna."

Again, no answer.

"This is very strange."

Matteo opened the door onto a cave which was completely empty except for a sofa and a TV set.

"Where's Father Pietro?" Roberto asked with frustration.

Matteo scratched his head. "This is the only place my family uses for hiding people. Then they have nothing to do with Father Pietro's disappearance."

"If neither of your families have taken Father Pietro, then who has?" Roberto asked.

Loretta plonked herself on the sofa. "I'm too tired."

Matteo sat next to her and draped his arm around her. "I'm sorry it's so difficult for us to be together."

"It's not your fault."

He kissed her forehead, she kissed him back, and as the kissing didn't stop, Roberto coughed pointedly.

"Shall we resume our search?" Roberto suggested.

"If he hasn't been taken by our families, we don't know where to start looking for him," Loretta said, nestling in Matteo's embrace.

"We can't even be sure that Father Pietro hasn't left of his own accord. He could have got fed up of all the church work and wanted some rest," Matteo said hopefully.

Right now Roberto could fully empathise with that feeling. But no, Father Pietro was a dedicated and conscientious parish priest. He would never abandon his flock and his coworker in the middle of the night, without a word.

Roberto suddenly stopped pacing the room. "I know what to do."

***

"We can't ask our families!" Loretta protested, getting up from the sofa. "As soon as we turn on our phones, they will be able to track where we are."

"I expect they have worked out where you are," Roberto ventured.

She paced the cave. "If we ask after Father Pietro, we'll confirm their suspicions that we want to get married."

"I imagine that those suspicions have already been confirmed."

"It makes perfect sense, Loretta," Matteo said. "Our families wouldn't hide him somewhere you or I know about. They must have taken him somewhere new."

"We should sleep on this," Loretta said.

Roberto checked his watch. Soon he would have to celebrate the morning Mass. "There isn't any sleeping time left."

"Let's go home," Matteo said, standing up.

"Okay," Loretta said.

Roberto couldn't believe that Matteo and Loretta had finally agreed to go home and talk to their parents. "Thank you!"

"We mean your home, Father."

***

Roberto woke up with a start when the car stopped in front of the church's garage. He felt guilty for falling asleep when Father Pietro was still missing.

Not only had they failed to find him, but they'd consumed his fuel and punctured his tyre, Roberto thought grimly as they stepped out of Father Pietro's car.

Back upstairs in the presbytery, Roberto was trying to work out how to accommodate an unmarried couple in a flat with only one spare room, when Loretta called out from the kitchen.

"There's a note!"

Roberto ran to see it.

Put together with newspaper cuttings, the message read: *Give us back our children if you want to see your friend again.*

"It's an exchange of hostages!" Loretta exclaimed.

"But the only hostage is Father Pietro," Roberto said, confused.

"Someone must have seen you take us away in Father Pietro's car and thought you were kidnapping us," Matteo explained.

"But I wasn't even driving!" Roberto

protested. If anyone was being held hostage, it was him.

"You could be pointing a gun to Loretta's back through the car seat," Matteo explained as if it was obvious.

Roberto shook his head. These people lived in a different world, one he might never fully understand.

Loretta put her hands to her heart. "Our families have written this note together! How lovely! You won't hand us over to them, will you, Father?" Loretta pleaded.

Until now, Roberto hadn't even thought he could do that. But there was a phone number at the bottom of the note.

"Our families are collaborating only because they have a common goal—to get us back," Matteo told him. "But as soon as you hand us over, their alliance will stop and they'll be at loggerheads again."

"And they'll stop us getting married or even seeing each other ever again," Loretta added with anguish.

Roberto thought for a moment. The thwarted lovers had come to him to be married in secret presumably because their families were not going to separate them once they were married.

"Then we will tell them that you're already

married."

Loretta and Matteo's eyes widened for a moment. They looked at each other, beaming.

"That's a great idea, Father!"

***

Roberto rang the number on the note and was told that someone would come and collect them. The exchange of "hostages" would take place in a secret location.

When some men turned up in a banged-up old car and informed Roberto, Matteo and Loretta that they had to be hooded, Roberto wondered if this was really an exchange of hostages or just the criminal families acquiring some more.

When the hoods finally came off, they were in a marble-floored room with chrome fittings, leather sofas and an enormous fish tank of tropical fish. This was clearly the home of someone rich and powerful.

The man who walked into the room had the hardened expression of a long-time criminal. Roberto hoped that the fish tank wasn't a symbol of his impending fate.

"Tonio Moneta!" Loretta gasped quietly.

This was the big boss. If the matter had escalated to him, Roberto's bluff was going to be even riskier. He clutched the rosary chain in his pocket.

"Please, take a seat," their host told them with surprising civility.

Roberto, Matteo and Loretta sat on the leather sofa. The young couple clasped each other's hands.

"I apologise for taking your colleague, Father," Tonio Moneta told Roberto. "I'm sure you'll understand that I couldn't run the risk that he'd marry the youngsters against my will."

"Why didn't you take me too?" Roberto asked.

Tonio gave him a pitiful look. "You weren't going to do anything without him."

Roberto couldn't deny that he was spot on.

Then Tonio turned to Loretta and Matteo. "I understand that you two would like to get married."

"Actually, we are already—" Matteo began but Roberto interrupted him.

"Yes, they would very much like to get married."

An inspiration had suddenly struck Roberto. He darted an apologetic glance at the couple for not following the plan they had agreed.

"With your consent, of course," Roberto continued.

The criminal boss grimaced. "That's very good," he said, which suggested that the grimace was a smile.

Roberto released a breath. His inspiration had been correct. He silently thanked God.

"I've been wanting to strike a peace deal with Ciccio Titotto for a while," Tonio explained, "but I can't have my people brokering their own deals with Ciccio's people without my approval."

Roberto nodded. "So do you give your consent to this marriage?"

"Yes, I do."

The beaming couple thanked the boss.

"Off you go to your families and don't cause trouble again," he warned.

Matteo and Loretta thanked Roberto with tears in their eyes and assured him that they would visit him soon to enrol in the marriage preparation course.

As they were escorted out, Tonio turned back to Roberto.

"Your boss is ready to go home. He's tired me so much that I've got to go to bed now."

He yawned.

∗∗∗

Roberto and Father Pietro were hooded again for the journey back, which was convenient because they both fell asleep at once.

They were dropped off at the bottom of the church's steps just as the first light of dawn glowed pink on the sandstone façade.

"I hope you were treated well," Roberto said to Father Pietro as soon as they were alone.

"Extremely well. Tonio Moneta kept me company the whole time."

"Was that a good thing?"

"Well, it started off as an interrogation. But once he was convinced that I didn't know anything about the couple, we talked about the origin of authority, the nature of power, and God."

"You evangelised Tonio Moneta?"

Father Pietro chuckled. "Not quite. Tonio still considers himself bigger than God, but he told me that he's interested in getting to know Him better and he'd like to have another chat with me soon."

"You'll go back to that place—with hoods, guns and all?"

"Of course."

"I admire you. You're so brave."

Father Pietro swatted the air. "Nonsense. I'm just older than you."

"How does that make you braver?"

"We humans live so long because we need time to grow into better people."

Roberto could think of several old people who had grown into more crotchety and unpleasant versions of themselves. Perhaps some folks didn't realise the opportunity they'd been given. He would do his absolute best to grow into a better version of himself.

"You must be hungry. Would you like something to eat?" he asked Father Pietro.

"Oh, no, I'm not hungry at all," Father Pietro said with a chuckle. "I was stuffed full of delicious food. Tonio is very fond of certain doughnuts as big as tyres, and he kept offering them to me. It would have been rude to refuse."

The mention of tyres reminded Roberto of something he had pushed out of his mind. Sooner or later he would have to own up to it with Father Pietro, so he might as well do it now.

"When we were looking for you, we took your car and, unfortunately, we had a puncture. We changed the wheel to the spare one but I guess the punctured one will need repairing now," Roberto told him ruefully.

"This is excellent news!" Father Pietro exclaimed, beaming.

"What do you mean?"

"I've always been afraid of getting a puncture because I had no idea how to change a tyre and I had no one to teach me. But as you know how to do it, now you can teach me! Just perfect!"

Roberto chuckled. Nothing could chip Father Pietro's cheerfulness.

That morning they opened the church as normal and resumed their parish duties as if nothing had happened. At the end of that very long day, Father Pietro went to bed early while Roberto popped down to the empty church for a quick bedtime prayer. He prayed for Loretta and Matteo, Tonio Moneta, and for himself—that he could be a little more like Father Pietro. Then he went back upstairs, checked that Father Pietro was still tucked in his bed, and slipped into his own—wonderful—bed, where he fell asleep at once.

The End

Other books by Stefania Hartley

In this series:

Father Roberto and the Missing Money
Father Roberto and the Rural Riots
Father Roberto and the Mystery of the
Microscope

Collections of short stories:

Tales from the Parish
Good Habits
Sweet Surprises
The Season to Be Jolly
Welcome to Quayside
Sand, Sea & Tamburello
A Season of Goodwill
To Be Loved
Drive Me Crazy
Stars Are Silver
Keeping it Cool
Fresh from the Sea
Confetti and Lemon Blossom
A Slip of the Tongue
What's Yours is Mine

Short Romances:

How to Choose a Husband
The Italian Fake Date
Sweet Competition for Camillo's Café
Second Chances at Mamma's Trattoria
Under Far Eastern Skies

ABOUT THE AUTHOR

Stefania was born in Sicily and immediately started growing, but not very much. She left her sunny island after falling head over heels in love with an Englishman, and now she lives in the UK with her husband and their three children. Having finally learnt English, she's enjoying it so much that she now writes novels and short stories which have been longlisted, shortlisted, commended, and won prizes.

If you have enjoyed these stories, please leave a review. To be the first to hear when she's releasing a new book, sign up for her newsletter and you'll receive an exclusive short story: www.stefaniahartley.com/subscribe